Ladybird Books Inc., Auburn, Maine 04210, U.S.A.
Published by Ladybird Books Ltd., Loughborough, Leicestershire, U.K.

Printed in Hong Kong

Birthday Bear

Georgina Russell
illustrated by Jenny Press

"That's the end of your story, Sally," said Mom. "Now snuggle down with Bear and go to sleep."

"I'm too excited to sleep," replied Sally. "I can't wait till tomorrow."

"I know," said Mom. "There are going to be lots of surprises."

Bear listened with sudden interest. Surprises! He liked surprises, too.

Sally lay awake for a long time, tossing and turning and thinking and wondering. But at last she drifted off to sleep.

Bear, however, was still doing a lot of thinking and wondering of his own.

As soon as everyone was safely asleep, Bear slipped out of Sally's arms and slid down onto the floor.

"I'll start with the closet under the stairs," he said to himself. "That's a good hiding place for surprises."

It was dark and crowded in the closet, so Bear had to rummage around with his paws.

"Coats and scarves, boots and shoes, cans of old paint, umbrellas…" muttered Bear. "But no sign of any surprises."

He rummaged some more. "Brushes and brooms, a teapot, a beach ball, an old hat…

Oh! And a big package wrapped in pretty paper and tied with a ribbon!"

Bear paused.

"A package… Packages mean presents, and presents mean surprises. So this *must* be a surprise," he decided.

He looked longingly
at the package,
wondering
what was
inside.

But Bear didn't open the package. "If I open it, it won't be a surprise any more," he said to himself. So, reluctantly, he turned away from the closet.

"Maybe I'll look in the kitchen next," he decided. "There might be an eating sort of surprise in there."

In the kitchen, Bear tried the cupboards first.

"Pots and pans, bowls and plates, cups and saucers, but no surprises," he said sadly to himself.

Next he tried the refrigerator.

"Butter and milk, yogurt and eggs, tomatoes and lettuce…

Oh! And a huge cake covered in pink icing with sugar teddy bears dancing around the side!"

Bear thought for a moment.

"A special cake... Special cakes with pink icing mean special occasions, and special occasions mean surprises. So this *must* be a surprise!" he decided.

But Bear was puzzled. "What *is* the special occasion?" he wondered.

Bear thought and thought. "I give up," he said to himself at last. "I'd better look in the dining room next. There may be a clue in there."

Bear pushed open the door and looked around.

"Table and chairs, knives and forks, plates and glasses. No surprises here."

He looked again.

"Oh! And balloons and funny hats!"

Bear thought for a moment.

"Balloons and funny hats mean parties, and parties mean special occasions, and special occasions mean surprises. But *what* is the special occasion?"

Bear sat down and thought even harder.

"It can't be Christmas – I haven't seen a Christmas tree…"

He thought some more. "I wonder if it's… could it be…?" Suddenly Bear tingled with excitement.

"Yes! That's it!" he said, jumping up. "It must be… it's got to be… my birthday! And Sally and her mom want it to be a surprise for me!"

Bear smiled a big smile as
he climbed the stairs. "I'd better
get to bed now," he thought.
"Tomorrow is going to be a big
day for me."

Next afternoon,
Bear watched as
Sally put on…

her party dress…

and party shoes.

He was bursting with anticipation.

"My big moment," thought Bear as Sally carried him downstairs.

The dining room was full of children wearing the funny hats and playing with the balloons. Oh! And there on the table Bear could see the wrapped-up present.

Next to it was the cake with pink icing and sugar teddy bears dancing around the side.

"That's funny!" thought Bear, as he counted the candles on the cake. "I didn't know I was five."

At that moment, all the children started singing:

"Happy Birthday to you,
Happy Birthday to you."

Bear listened happily.

"Happy Birthday, dear Sally,
Happy Birthday to you."

Bear couldn't believe his ears. It was *Sally's* birthday, not his. This was the wrong sort of surprise! It was awful.

All the children were laughing and shouting. Sally was smiling. Bear felt disappointed, sad, and forgotten.

Then all at once Sally announced, "I'm going to blow out the candles. And my special friend Bear is going to help me!"

She tied the ribbon from the package in a big bow around his neck, and gave him a pink party hat.

Bear brightened up. He hadn't been forgotten, after all!

Sally took a big breath. So did Bear.

All five candles went out with one puff. Or was it two?

"Happy Birthday, Sally!" cried the children. "Hooray, Bear!"

Bear grinned to himself. He felt very handsome in his party hat and bow. And he felt very proud to be Sally's special friend. It was a happy surprise after all!